The Four Singers

Retold by Haydn Middleton

Illustrated by Seb Burnett

Once upon a time, there was a hard-working donkey called Tip Top. For many years Tip Top carried sacks of corn for the miller. But then he grew old and weak.

"I need a new donkey," the miller told his wife. "Tip Top will have to be sold."

Now Tip Top didn't like the sound of that! If he couldn't carry sacks, he wanted to be a singer. So he ran off as fast as his legs could carry him.

On the road Tip Top met a hungry old dog by the name of Lickety Split.

"I'm too old for hunting now," Lickety Split told Tip Top. "So my master plans to get rid of me."

"Then run away with me," said Tip Top.
"But who will give us food?" asked Lickety Split.
"We'll sing to people and they will give us food in return!" said Tip Top.
That sounded very tasty to Lickety Split.

Soon, Tip Top and Lickety Split came across a sleepy old cat.

"I've grown far too slow to catch mice," said Scatty Cat – for that was the sleepy cat's name. "Now my mistress wants to throw me out!"

"Can you sing?" asked Lickety Split.

Scatty Cat miaowed loudly.

"Come and join us!" said Tip Top.

"We're going to sing songs in return for food," Lickety Split explained.

"Whatever you say," said Scatty Cat, sleepily.

The three singers came to a farmyard. There they found a proud old cockerel called Doodle Doo.

"How well you sing," Lickety Split said to him. "I do everything well," Doodle Doo replied. "Yet the farmer's wife plans to eat me!"

"Then come and join our singing group," said Scatty Cat with a yawn.

"We'll sing for our supper!" said Lickety Split.

"Very well," said Doodle Doo. "But I shall be your lead singer."

Night fell and the four singers came to a house in the forest. They looked through the window.

"Some robbers live in this house," said Tip Top.

"All robbers like good music!" said Doodle Doo.
"Let us sing for them!"

"And then they will give us food," added Lickety Split.

So Lickety Split climbed onto Tip Top's back.

Scatty Cat climbed onto Lickety Split's back.

And last, but not least, Doodle Doo perched on Scatty Cat's head.

Then they all started to sing.
What a din they made!

Scatty Cat
miaowed.

Lickety Split
howled.

Tip Top
brayed.

And Doodle Doo crowed for all he was worth.

The robbers screamed. They thought a monster had come to kill them. In panic, they all ran out of the house and deep into the forest.

The four singers went in through the open door and they found enough food for four lifetimes.

They ate until they could eat no more. Then they put out the lights and fell asleep.

Meanwhile, deep in the forest, the captain of the robbers had a plan.

"Go back to the house now," he said to the smallest robber. "See if the monster has gone."

The smallest robber tiptoed back to the house.
He found no monster outside, so in he went and
lit a candle.

But the sudden light woke all the singers.
"We're in danger!" they thought.
So what did each one do?

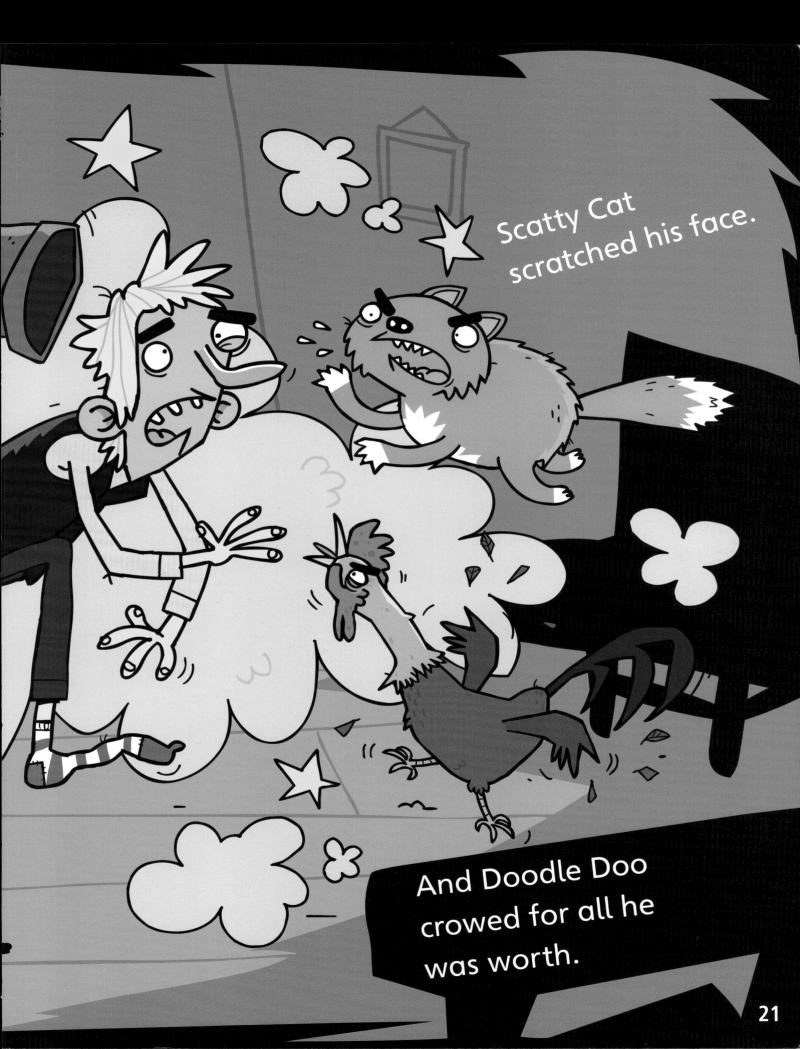

Scatty Cat scratched his face.

And Doodle Doo crowed for all he was worth.

21

The robber raced back to his captain. "The monster is in our house now," panted the robber. "And it can kick, bite, scratch and crow all at the same time!"

With that, every single robber screamed in terror and fled – never to return.

"Let's stay here in this house forever,"
said the four singers.
And they struck up a song of pure joy!